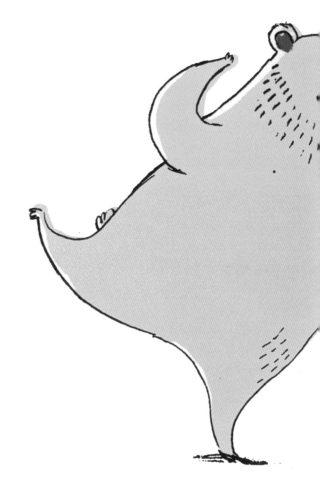

For **Alice**
who always saves me from my bad ideas
F.S.

DAISY AND BEAR
SCENE1 TAKE 1

First published in 2019 by Scholastic Children's Books
Euston House, 24 Eversholt Street, London NW1 1DB
a division of Scholastic Ltd
www.scholastic.co.uk

London ~ New York ~ Toronto ~ Sydney ~ Auckland ~ Mexico City ~ New Delhi ~ Hong Kong

Text and illustrations copyright © 2019 Fabi Santiago

Edited by Pauliina Malinen • Designed by Strawberrie Donnelly

ISBN 978 1407 18669 6

DAISY and BEAR

WORDS AND PICTURES BY FABI SANTIAGO

SCHOLASTIC

On Sunday afternoons, Daisy and I just take it easy.
But today, Daisy had a brilliant idea.
"Let's go to the **cinema!**" she said.

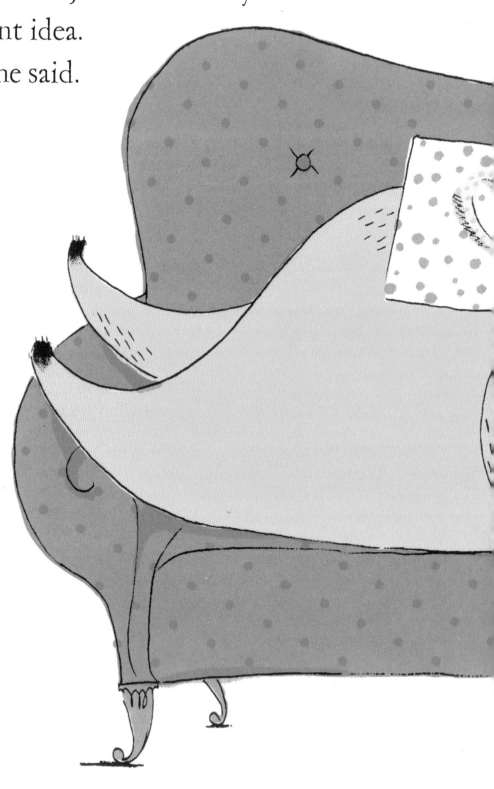

Daisy laughed.
"Bear, have you NEVER been to the cinema?"

"Cinema,"
Daisy explained, "is where you go and watch a **film** with lots of other people on a GIANT screen ...

... and there are hundreds of soft comfy seats and big velvet curtains and warm popcorn and ..."

When we got to the cinema, I couldn't even count
all the people as I only count up to eleven.
"This is the **queue,**" said Daisy. "We'll have to do a teensy bit of waiting."

~ But waiting
is BORING!

We peeked inside, and I couldn't
believe it. The cinema was ...

...amazing!

I loved it already.

I went upstairs ...

... and down again.

It wasn't **much** trouble, really, and I got us some treats too.

I have to say, I am brilliant at watching films.

Daisy didn't think so. "Shhh Bear, you need to be QUIET!"

GUESS what just happened?

Everyone was having a **great** time.

But Daisy was suddenly in a rush to leave.

Maybe SHE needed the loo now, too?

"Bear, listen!" said Daisy.
"This is a CINEMA. You can't just ..."

Daisy sounded serious.
Clearly, she needed more popcorn,
so I decided to top up our treats.

~ I wonder what this button does?

That button did ... a LOT!

I had ruined the film for everyone.

I should never have set a paw in the cinema.

"Don't worry, Bear," said Daisy. "These things happen."

But they always happen to ME!

I wasn't sad for long ...

... because I had a
fantastic idea.

Follow me, Daisy! ~

BACKSTAGE →

"Bear...?"

We were the **stars** of the show!
There was clapping.
There was cheering.
There was free popcorn!

Bearlissimo!

BIG SHOW

FREE POPCORN

Bravo!

Daisy giggled.
"And we love YOU, Bear!"

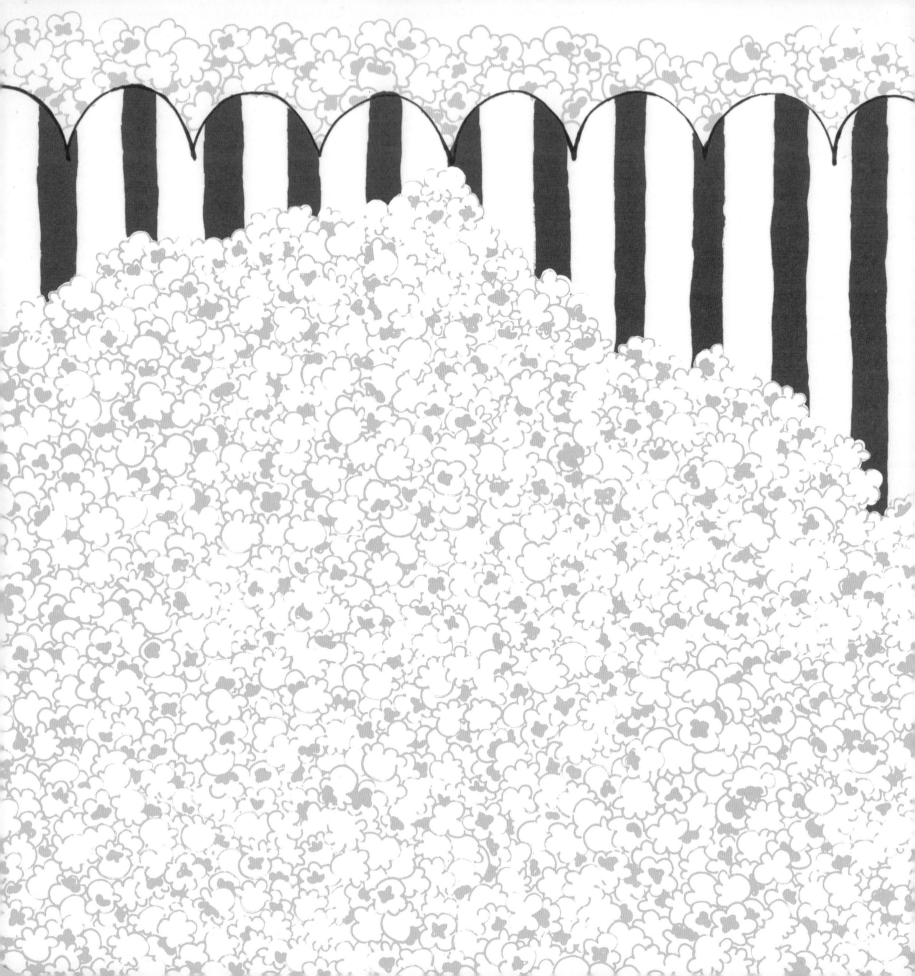

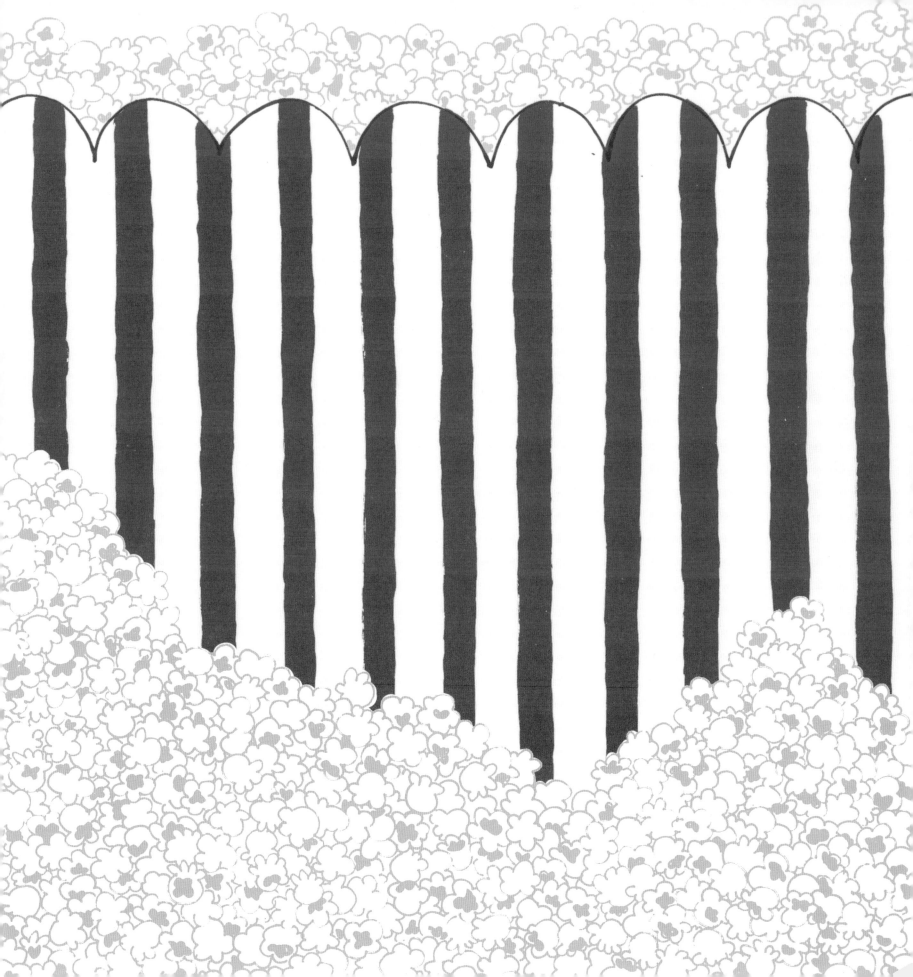